Meg Cabot has lived in Indiana and California, USA, and in France. She has worked as an assistant dorm manager of a large university, an illustrator and a writer of historical romance (under a different name). She currently lives in New York City with her husband and a one-eyed cat called Henrietta, and says she is still waiting for her real parents, the king and queen, to come and restore her to her rightful throne.

The Walt Disney Pictures feature film based on *The Princess Diaries* was hugely successful and the sequel is about to be released.

Visit Meg Cabot's website at
www.megcabot.com

The SECRET PRINCESS DIARIES

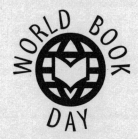

WORLD BOOK DAY

Thursday **6th March 2003**
www.worldbookday.com

Meg Cabot

Specially published for WBD 2003

MACMILLAN

To all the little princesses out there

First published 2003 by Macmillan Children's Books
a division of Macmillan Publishers Limited
20 New Wharf Road, London N1 9RR
Basingstoke and Oxford
www.panmacmillan.com

Associated companies throughout the world

ISBN 0 330 41814 9

1 3 5 7 9 8 6 4 2

A CIP catalogue record for this book is available from
the British Library.

Printed and bound in Great Britain by Mackays of Chatham plc, Kent

Wednesday, March 9, Limo home from the Plaza Hotel

IT IS SO UNFAIR!!!!!!!!!!

I don't know why, just because I happen to have had the misfortune to have been born a princess – even though I was not aware of it until recently – that I must be PENALIZED for it by my own relations. Don't they know that by stifling my growth as an individual in this manner, they are probably going to cause me to have deep-seated problems later in life?

I mean, it is bad enough that they waited until I was nearly fifteen before letting me in on the whole, 'Oh-by-the-way-you're-a-princess' thing. And Dad thinks the fact that he's even letting me stay in school instead of shipping me off to Genovia for the rest of my life is like this huge concession. Except that hello, Dad, you can't have it both ways. You can't tell a person she's a princess, then let her stay in ninth grade with her friends like a normal person, then suddenly be all, 'Oh, no, wait, you can't do that, you're a princess,' when she wants to do something every normal ninth-grader in America should get to do.

I mean, this could drive even a reasonably adjusted person insane. And I am not even close to being reasonably adjusted.

I asked Grandmere about it at our princess lesson in her hotel suite this afternoon:

'Don't you realize that you are stifling my growth as an individual at a very crucial stage in my social development,' I asked, 'and that there is a strong likelihood I might grow up to have a split personality and turn into Tess of the D'Urbervilles at random, but crucial, moments such as when greeting dignitaries from foreign lands at state functions?'

But all Grandmere said was:

'Don't be ridiculous, Amelia. Besides, if you do turn out to have a split personality, I'm sure you'll come up with someone much more interesting to be than an itinerant maid. Mary Queen of Scots, I think, would be more the thing, or Elizabeth Taylor.'

Why was I cursed with having the meanest grandmother in the history of time? I mean, Lizzie Borden, who chopped up her parents with an axe, was probably meaner than Grandmere, but I really can't think of anyone who'd be worse. Besides, maybe Lizzie's parents deserved it, who knows? Maybe Lizzie, like me, asked if she could spend her Spring Break building homes for the volunteer organization Housing for the Homeless, and her parents, like mine, said no. Maybe her parents, like mine, said, 'No, I'm sorry, Lizzie, you have to spend Spring Break in

Genovia with your grandmother so that you can preside over the nine hundred and seventy-fifth anniversary of your ancestress Rosagunde strangling the life from the leader of a marauding band of Visigoths and making the Riviera safe so Angelina Jolie won't feel uncomfortable coming over for the Cannes Film Festival premiere of *Tomb Raider II*.'

You could see how that sort of thing might drive someone completely postal.

And OK, I wouldn't really want to chop my parents up with an axe because:

a. most of the time I like them, and I'd miss them if they were gone, and
b. excuse me, but gross. Couldn't Lizzie have thought of a less messy way to get rid of them? Like, couldn't she have called Child Protective Services or pushed them down a well, or whatever?

It is just so UNFAIR!!!! I mean, everyone in my whole school, practically, is going to West Virginia to build houses for the poor of the Appalachian Mountains – everyone except me. They are giving out ten whole points of extra credit to people who go. Ten points can mean the difference between a C and B! AND it looks good on your college applications, which is the only reason popular people like Lana Weinberger and Josh Richter, who have never so much as handed a homeless person a quarter in their lives, are going.

And they aren't the only ones: Lilly Moscovitz, my best friend and resident school genius, is going. Her boyfriend, Boris Pelkowski, violin virtuoso and mouth breather, is going, too. My own boyfriend, Lilly's older brother Michael, is going, and he doesn't even *need* extra credit. He is the senior class co-valedictorian. Even Tina Hakim Baba, whose father owns a bunch of oil wells and is always worried about Tina getting kidnapped by some rival oil baron's henchmen, is allowed to go.

BUT NOT ME!

I stressed to my dad that it was totally a school sanctioned outing, and would be fully supervised by Dr Juan Gonzales, the director of the Northeast Division of Housing for the Homeless; Albert Einstein High School's principal, Dr Gupta; Mrs Hill from my Gifted and Talented class (not that I am gifted *or* talented, but whatever); Mademoiselle Klein from French; and Mr Wheeton, the track coach and Health and Safety teacher. Oh, and, hello, the Appalachian Mountains are only, like, seven hours away from Manhattan by bus, and the whole trip is only for three days, so what is the BIG DEAL????

But Dad STILL said no.

THIS IS PRINCESS PREJUDICE, that's what

it is. A bias crime against me because of an accident of BIRTH! IT IS JUST PLAIN WRONG!

If I don't go completely Hannibal Lecter because of all of this, it will only be because I have suffered so many hardships throughout my fourteen and three quarters years. First the stigma of illegitimacy, due to the fact that my mother and father never cemented the bonds of their love in holy matrimony. But let us not forget the other traumas I have endured that have helped prepare me for a life of torment:

a. size ten feet
b. complete lack of body fat in chestal area
c. maths dyslexia (unproven at this point, but surely this is why at my age I still can't multiply fractions. I know they tested for this and it was proven that I don't have any learning disabilities, but haven't they learned by now that I don't test well?)
d. discovering that I am actually the heir to the throne of a small European country (population 50,000)
e. being forced to spend hours every day after school with my paternal grandmother as she prepares me for my eventual ascending the throne, tutoring me in such vitally important areas as cutlery arrangement and tiara-donning

e.   boyfriendless for first fourteen and one half
      years of my life (happily this is the one area
      which has seen some improvement of late)

Really, looking at this list, it is a wonder that I
have survived as long as I have. I didn't even
include the part about my mom being married to
my Algebra teacher and expecting to deliver his
baby in three months. I mean, how many other
ninth-grade girls actually sit around worrying
about their mother's elevated triglyceride levels, or
have the memory of seeing their Algebra teacher
in his underwear burned into their retinas?

Not many, I bet.

But oh, lucky me, I DO!!!!!!!!!!!!!

It's probably just as well that they won't let me
go. I mean, it's not like I actually know anything
about building houses. It's not like I am going to
be able to contribute anything to the Albert
Einstein High School student construction team,
considering that my hand–eye coordination is nil.
I mean, they probably wouldn't even want me,
considering what a talentless freak I am – except
maybe for the whole writing thing. But what
good is being able to *write*? I mean, entertain-
ingly? It would be so much cooler if I were skilled
at using a lathe, or something actually *useful* to
society.

But if I don't go to West Virginia, how am I

ever going to find out? About whether or not I am skilled with a lathe, I mean?

Maybe I should just go to Genovia with Grandmere and face the fact that the only thing I can do moderately well is write and possibly order in Chinese food, and that it is highly unlikely that I have some kind of hidden talent for hanging drywall and that I am going to discover it while building houses for the homeless over Spring Break.

There is no justice in the world.

Thursday, March 10, Homeroom

Last night I impressed upon my mother the importance of my going to West Virginia for Spring Break. I didn't mention the part about how if I end up in Genovia, I may never find out whether or not I have a secret gift for home construction. I didn't think this would impress my mother, who, being extremely talented herself, thinks people who don't have any talent worry too much about the whole thing.

Instead, I explained to her about the 'theology of the hammer' – how partnerships founded on common ground, for instance, a lot of people from different ethnic, religious, and socio-economic groups getting together to build a house, bridge theological differences by putting caring into action. I mentioned how everyone can use a hammer, turning it into an instrument that manifests peace and love.

My mom – who was lying on her bed watching *Stolen Women, Captured Hearts* on the Lifetime movie channel with a carton of Häagen-Dazs chocolate chocolate-chip ice-cream balanced on her enormous stomach, even though she is supposed to be limiting her saturated fat intake to less than twenty grams a day due to her more-than-thirty-pound weight gain in the past half a year – just looked at me and asked, 'Mia, are you in a cult?'

OH, MY GOD! Only the extreme hormonal imbalance my mother is going through right now could make her believe that my working to provide affordable housing for the poor, so that they can live in dignity and safety, is in any way comparable to religious fanaticism.

When I mentioned that out loud, however, my mother shrieked, 'Frank! Come here, quick! Mia's in a cult!'

Thank God Mr Gianini came into the bedroom – he'd been in the living room, practising his drums – and explained to my mother in a calm, reasonable voice that Housing for the Homeless is not a cult, that it is a non-profit, non-denominational organization dedicated to eliminating substandard housing and homelessness worldwide. He also said that he himself had volunteered to escort students from Albert Einstein the past five Spring Breaks, and that the only reason he hadn't gone this year was on account of my mom being pregnant with his unborn child, the sex of which we do not know because my mom says if she knows it's a boy she won't have any incentive to push, men being the reason we even need organizations like Housing for the Homeless, because male politicians make such bad decisions when they are elected to public office, such as paying for nuclear missile silos before making sure all their constituents have decent housing first, etc.

So then I looked at my mom with my eyes really big, the way Fat Louie's get when I give him the wrong flavour of Fancy Feast, and it must have worked a little since she went, 'Fine, I'll talk to your father. Get out of the way, you're blocking Janine Turner.'

So who knows???? Maybe I'll get to go to West Virginia after all!!!!!!!!!!!

Thursday, March 10, Gifted and Talented

Everyone in our entire Gifted and Talented class, including our teacher, Mrs Hill, is going to West Virginia, except for me. I mean, as I already mentioned, even *Boris Pelkowski* is going.

I am sorry, but if I were a poor person, I would NOT want Boris Pelkowski building a house for me. Even if the alternative was NO house, I would not want Boris building my house. I know Boris is the most gifted person in our whole Gifted and Talented class, but once during a school orchestra concert Boris went into the third floor stairwell so he could practise his solo in private and he ended up locking himself out and had to bang on the steel doors for hours before anyone found him. I mean, the concert had already ended by then, and everybody had gone home. It was lucky the custodian was still on duty or Boris might have been trapped in that stairwell all weekend. Without food or water, he might have died, and on Monday when everybody came back to school, all they'd have found was this skeleton clutching a violin and wearing a sweater tucked into its pants.

Lilly is so excited about the West Virginia trip, she can't talk about anything else. She is bringing her video camera, and she is going to tape the trip and show it later on her public access cable television programme, *Lilly Tells It Like It Is*. She says it is going to be a searing commentary on the inadequacies of our public housing system.

'It's a shame you aren't going with us, Mia,' Lilly just said to me. 'I heard Lana and Josh are planning on sitting in the back row of the bus and making out the entire time we're on the Jersey Turnpike. I was going to surreptitiously record their saliva swapping and present it on the next episode of my show as a part of a documentary on teen mating rituals.'

Nice of my best friend to be so sympathetic to my plight and not rub it in, or anything. I can't believe my parents won't let me go. I HATE being a princess. PRINCESSES MISS OUT ON EVERYTHING COOL!!!!!!!!!!

Thursday, March 10, After school, the Plaza Hotel

I CAN GO!!!!!!!!!!!!!!!!!!!!

It is a Spring Break miracle. The nine hundred and seventy-fifth anniversary of my ancestress Rosagunde's strangling of the Visigoth warlord who slayed her father and took over her village has been cancelled due to the fact that Monaco, Genovia's closest neighbour, is hosting a Bruce Springsteen concert THAT VERY DAY, and who in their right mind would rather go to some dumb anniversary celebration than see Springsteen live?

Grandmere is way burnt up about the whole thing – she thinks Bruce did it on purpose. 'It would be so like him,' she keeps saying.

I refuse to believe my grandmother has ever met Bruce Springsteen. Yo-Yo Ma I can believe. But the Boss?

'I suppose it's just as well,' Grandmere said philosophically, taking a long pull at her Gitane. 'I need a little R and R myself. Do you think it's easy, teaching a young girl, day in, day out, everything she needs to know in order to rule a country someday? *Pfuit!* Not at all. I am going to Palm Springs for a mudbath and some Swedish massage. At least there I can enjoy a cigarette

13

without hearing about how I am destroying the environment and the lungs of all those around me with my secondhand smoke,' she added, with an evil look in my direction.

But I don't care, because it means I am FREE!!!!!! FREE TO GO TO WEST VIRGINIA WITH MY BEST FRIEND, HER BOYFRIEND and, best of all, MY BOYFRIEND!!!!!!!!

Appalachian Mountains, here I come!!!!!!!!!

Friday, March 11, Lunch meeting of the Albert Einstein High School Housing for the Homeless Brigade

I am having grave reservations about West Virginia. I mean, I know there are poor people there and all, but it is still in AMERICA, for crying out loud.

But Dr Gonzales just gave us this list of things we need to bring with us, and Lilly and Michael and Boris and Tina and I are just sitting here, reading it, going, hello, is this a joke? Like what is a five-gallon solar shower-bag? Where would you even buy one of those? And what is with the potassium-rich, non-melting snack items? What are THOSE? What are we going to need potassium for? Don't they have grocery stores in West Virginia? I mean, can't we just go to the deli and buy a banana?

Other things we are supposed to bring include:
Tool belt or cloth nail pouch
Hammer with claw
Gloves for handling rough lumber, hammers, shovels, etc.
25–30ft tape measure
Utility knife
Wire cutter and/or tin snips to cut the chicken and bailing wire

Small nail puller or cat's claw
Carpenter's pencil
Small square: combo, tri or carpenter's
Sharp, small (short shank) hand saw
Chalk line (optional)

Um, hello. I am a princess. I don't have any of these things. Need a sceptre? Hey, yeah, I'm your girl. Nail puller? Not so much.

And, hello again, you would think they would give us some lessons on like gypsum board or whatever, but no. Instead, Dr Gonzales just gave us these release forms that our parents are supposed to sign, saying that they won't hold Housing for the Homeless responsible in the event that we are maimed or killed on the trip.

Maimed or killed!!!!!

Lana Weinberger just raised her hand and wanted to know why the handout says we need to bring a week's supply of Wet Wipes with us. Dr Gonzales says because on cloudy days, our five-gallon solar shower-bags might not warm up enough and so we should be prepared either to take a cold shower or use Wet Wipes to clean ourselves. Now Lana looks like somebody just told her she's going to be expected to eat full-fat yogurt.

Ha ha! Lana might not be able to wash her precious golden locks for three whole days in a row!

I stopped smirking when Dr Gonzales asked us

all to turn to Page Two of the handout. That's because Page Two said:

Drink plenty of sports drinks, Gatorade or cranberry juice the week prior to departing. Drink the Gatorade provided at the worksite to raise your electrolyte and potassium levels.

There are a great many flying insects in this climate, you will need insect repellant.

Don't pet the local animals since they often carry diseases. Wash your hands immediately if you do.

Don't drink the shower water or water from the local spigots.

Don't drink the water or pet the animals? Insect repellant? Gatorade?

Oh, my God, what have I got myself into??????

Friday, March 11, Princess Lesson, the Plaza Hotel

Grandmere read over the release forms and told me she hoped I'd have fun in boot camp.

'It's not boot camp, Grandmere,' I told her. 'It's a non-profit, non-denominational organization dedicated to eliminating substandard housing and homelessness worldwide.'

'Then why,' Grandmere wanted to know, 'does it say here that you will need to rise every morning at six a.m.?'

'Because,' I said, snatching the forms back from her. 'That's probably when they serve breakfast.'

Grandmere shook her head. 'The last time I got up at six a.m. was when the Germans were shelling the palace, back during the war. Nothing short of anti-aircraft fire should get a princess out of bed before eight. Anything earlier is indecent. It is not too late, Amelia, for you to join me in Palm Springs. Are you sure you don't want to come? There's no need to wear insect repellant in the desert. And there won't be any Wet Wipes, just the beautiful crystal waters of the hotel pool, and Belgian waffles from room service . . .'

'No!' I yelled, because the waffle part sounded really tempting. I bet nobody at the spa where

Grandmere is going has to worry about their potassium levels. 'I am going to spend my Spring Break doing something good for mankind.' And, hopefully, discovering that I am a skilled shingle layer. Hey, you never know. 'Remember Prince William? He spent a YEAR after high school in Chile helping the poor. I'm just going to West Virginia, and only for three days. I think I can hold out for three days of getting up at six a.m.'

Grandmere just took a sip of her Sidecar and petted Rommel, her hairless miniature poodle.

'Suit yourself,' she said. 'But I hope this doesn't mean you are going to start going about in native wear, like those bulky Chilean sweaters Prince William started wearing. You know how wool gives you a rash.'

I told Grandmere they don't wear sweaters in West Virginia, and she asked what they do wear, then, and I had to admit I didn't know. That's when she stabbed a finger at me and went, 'Ah ha! I'll tell you what they wear in West Virginia! Gunnysacks! That's what they wear in West Virginia!'

I told Grandmere that, contrary to what she might believe, the Depression is over and nobody wears gunnysacks any more.

But I don't know. I mean, what about that movie *Nell* starring Jody Foster, where she played that deaf-mute who lived way out in the woods and was always going on about 'dancin' een the weend'? I am pretty sure that was set in West Virginia. And she was wearing a gunnysack. Or a housedress at the very least.

Oh, my God, I hope they don't expect us to dress like the natives in order to blend in! I don't own a housedress! I don't even think you can buy one of those in New York!

Friday, March 11, 11 p.m., The Loft

I was so worked up about all the gunnysacks and Gatorade that when I got home I asked Mr Gianini if there was something he maybe wasn't telling me about his past trips with Housing for the Homeless. Mr G has never actually been to West Virginia before, but he went to Mexico and some Texas border towns with H for the H. He went, 'Really, Mia, I can't say enough positive things about the experience. It really taught me to appreciate all that I have.'

Which is fine, but didn't really answer my question about the gunnysacks. He did say I could borrow his hammer though.

So I went online and instant messaged Michael, because, after all, he is my heart's desire and the only person on earth who can soothe me when my soul turns as fractious as an injured pony.

But even though he is my reason for living and all of that, Michael was totally unhelpful about the whole gunnysack thing.

LinuxRulz: Mia, the people we are going to build homes for are poor, not demented. I am sure they are going to be wearing something other than bags. I

mean, it's not going to be like in
Deliverance.

I have never seen *Deliverance* because I don't like movies where things jump out at people from behind trees, but I pretended like I had because I want Michael to think I am mature for my age. After all, he is a senior and I am only a freshman. I have to do what I can to keep him from remembering I am only fourteen and three quarters years old.

FtLouie: I know. But I mean, did you ever read *Christy*?

This is kind of a stupid question to ask a guy, since the only guy I know who has read *Christy* is my neighbour Ronnie, who is now a girl. But whatever. Michael is way well read, for a member of what my mom likes to call the cult of patriarchy.

FtLouie: Because *Christy* takes place in the Smoky Mountains, which are like the Appalachians, and everybody in it gets typhoid because of the insanitary conditions, including Christy, and I am just saying, maybe that's why we're not supposed to touch the animals . . .
>

22

LinuxRulz: Mia, stop worrying so much.
If it were really unsafe, do you think
Principal Gupta would be going?

FtLouie: Principal Gupta does some very
strange things sometimes. Remember when
she agreed to play Officer Krupke in the
Drama Club's production of *West Side
Story*?
>
LinuxRulz: Mia, instead of obsessing over
the possibility of contracting typhoid
and/or having to wear a gunnysack, why
don't you try to keep in mind the most
important aspect of this whole trip?

I thought maybe he meant the whole thing
where I might possibly find out that I am good at
something besides recording every single last
detail of my existence in this diary, which is not
exactly a worthwhile skill. But then I realized he
couldn't possibly mean that, because I hadn't
mentioned my secret fantasy that it turns out I
am an excellent plasterer or whatever. So instead
I wrote:

FtLouie: You mean the part where we are
helping the poor to self-actualize?
>

LinuxRulz: No, I mean the part where you and I get to spend three whole days together without any interference from your grandmother.

Ooooh! I'd forgotten about that!

Michael's right. Who cares about typhoid when there's *kissing*?

Saturday, March 12, 5:30 a.m., On the bus to West Virginia

Well, the kissing hasn't started yet.

That's because before we'd even got to the Lincoln Tunnel, Boris got carsick and had to throw up in a paper bag, and Lilly said no way was she sitting by him any more, and told Michael to move so she could sit by me, and when Michael said no, Boris threw up some more, only this time he missed the paper bag, and it went all over the floor, and Principal Gupta and Mrs Hill had to clean it up, but they didn't do a very good job on account of not having any paper towels or anything, so we all had to move to the back of the bus, away from the vomit fumes, and Michael was the only one who volunteered to stay with Boris and make sure next time he threw up in the bag.

My boyfriend is so cool. Not only is he incredibly smart and a very talented musician and skilled with computers and all of that, but he is also extremely compassionate. Maybe he will be a doctor, some day, and discover a cure for cancer. I certainly hope so, because that's the only way the Genovian Parliament is going to approve me marrying him.

I am not worried, though. Michael is a man

amongst men, and will doubtless do something extraordinary with his life that will win the hearts of the Genovian people, just as he has won mine. If only I had as many useful talents as Michael does. It would be nice if I could play the guitar *and* knew html.

Anyway, even though I offered to sit up in the front of the bus with Michael and help him pass paper bags to Boris, he said, just like Daniel Day Lewis in *Last of the Mohicans*, 'No, Mia, save yourself,' so now Lilly, Tina and I are all crammed into one seat until we get to the first rest stop on the Turnpike and the bus driver can give the floor a good hosing. Principal Gupta says as soon as we pull over, she is going to buy some Dramamine and make Boris take it. Boris says Dramamine makes him drowsy and robs him of his personality.

I can't wait.

Anyway, Lilly has already started filming. She got a very good close-up of the vomit. She started filming at five a.m., which is the time everybody had to be at Albert Einstein High School with all of our stuff in order to catch the bus. Everybody had a lot of stuff, especially considering that this trip will only last three days (not counting the day we arrive and the day we leave).

The winner of the most luggage award was Lana. She arrived with like five giant suitcases.

All of them in leopard print. I tried to get Grandmere to let me buy leopard print luggage once, and she was all, 'You are not Anna Nicole Smith.'

The person with the least luggage is my bodyguard, Lars. All he brought is one small duffel bag. I asked Lars where his sleeping bag and pillow were, and he just smiled. I hope he does not think he is sharing mine. I love my bodyguard, but not that much.

Anyway, Lilly is filming everything on the bus so we won't forget a thing. She took a good long shot of the sign hanging over the bus driver's head. The sign says:

> *I am your bus driver,* Charlie.
> *Safe, courteous, and reliable.*
> *Please stay back behind the yellow line.*

While we were stuck in traffic in front of the Lincoln Tunnel, Lilly asked us what we thought Charlie would do if Principal Gupta suddenly threw herself across the yellow line.

'Because Charlie is safe and reliable,' Tina said, 'he would probably go, *Miss! Stay back behind the yellow line!*'

'Yes,' I agreed. 'But because he is also courteous, he'd probably put it like, *Please, miss! Stay back behind the yellow line! Thank you!*'

27

Lana, who was fully eavesdropping on our conversation, leaned over the back of our seat and went, 'Could you guys *be* bigger dorks?'

Then Tina went, 'Dorks, *thank you*,' because she was imitating Charlie the bus driver, and we all about died laughing. Well, except for Lana and Josh, who just looked at us like we were insane.

I think maybe we are. Maybe it's the vomit fumes.

Only six and a half more hours to go until we get there.

Saturday, March 12, 10 a.m.,
Somewhere along Interstate Highway 78

Michael and I are finally sitting together but, unlike some people, we are not making out because Michael does not believe in public displays of affection, because, as he says, Some Things Are Private.

Which I fully understand and appreciate. I mean, it is not like I want him to go around Frenching me in the caf, or whatever. But you know, *holding hands* wouldn't hurt.

On the other hand, it is sort of uncomfortable to hold hands for any extended period of time. Mine always start getting all sweaty. My hands, I mean. Michael's don't. His hands are never sweaty. Maybe on account of him being a musician and all.

Maybe I am suffering from a genetic mutation. I mean, on top of my flat-chestedness and lack-of-useful-skill-ism. Maybe I've got an extra sweaty-hand chromosome, or something.

Anyway, Charlie, being safe, courteous and reliable, hosed down Boris's barf when we got to the Molly Pitcher Service Area, and then we all got back on board, and with the windows down, you really can't smell it that much. Principal Gupta gave Boris a good dose of Dramamine,

29

and now he is unconscious with his head lolling against Lilly's shoulder. I guess he wasn't kidding about motion sickness medicine causing him to lose his personality. We should give him some every day, if you ask me.

The only people on the bus who have been caught making out so far are, not surprisingly, Josh and Lana. They were first spotted sucking face in the Roy Rogers at the rest stop, but a sharp rebuke from Principal Gupta caused them to spring apart.

But just recently I looked towards the back of the bus, and they were at it again! Those two can't keep their hands off each other!!! It is truly sick.

Oh, my God, I am so tired. I can't wait until we get there, and all the kissing can start.

Saturday, March 12, 5 p.m., Hominy Knob, West Virginia

Oh . . . my . . . God.

We're here. We finally arrived. We finally arrived, and Charlie unloaded our bags, and then we had to pick them up and carry them to . . .

OUR TENTS!!!!!!!!!!!!

YES!!!!!!!!!!!!!!!! TENTS!!!!!!!!!! WE ARE SUPPOSED TO STAY IN TENTS!!!!!!!!!!

I have never slept in a tent in my life. Seriously, I am not trying to be a princess about this, but TENTS?????????? I mean, what about bears? And don't tell me there are no bears around here, because we are SURROUNDED by woods, there is NOTHING but woods in West Virginia, and yeah, Principal Gupta keeps going on about how beautiful it is, and look at the mountains and smell the clean fresh air, but hello???? BEARS!!!!!!!!

And didn't she ever see *The Blair Witch Project*? I mean, I will admit I watched that entire movie with my eyes closed, but it SOUNDED really scary, and I believe it took place, um, where? OH YES, THE WOODS!!!!!!!!!

That is it. We are all so dead.

Lars says not to worry, that he will make sure no wild animals or serial killers get into the tent Lilly, Tina and I are sharing. But I don't know.

That's what the people in *The Blair Witch Project* did, and look what happened to them! All they found of that one guy was his finger! I do not want to find Lars's finger! I do not want to lose Lars, he is an excellent bodyguard with a good sense of humour. Plus he doesn't mind when Michael and I kiss. Do you know how rare that is in a bodyguard????

Anyway, West Virginia itself isn't so bad. So far we haven't met one person wearing a gunnysack or playing the banjo in a menacing way. Everybody looks . . . well, just like people in New York. We haven't met our 'host family' yet. The way it works is, we are all split into groups, and then each group is assigned to a host family, and then they work on that family's house. I was very scared about the group thing, like that I might get assigned to a group away from all my friends, where I wouldn't know anybody. Or worse, a group with Lana in it. But fortunately, you get to pick your own group. So Michael, Lilly, Boris, Tina, Mrs Hill, Lars, me, Dr Gonzales and this one boy, Peter Tsu, who is a junior and is on the wrestling team, are all in one group.

I feel kind of sorry for our host family, to tell you the truth. Because I mean except for Dr Gonzales and possibly Peter Tsu, who I don't know anything about, none of us have ever built anything before. Some of us have never even held a hammer before.

Our host family's house has a fair chance of ending up looking like complete crud.

Oh, God, there's the bell. We are supposed to gather in the 'dining tent' now for orientation and supper. I am having grave reservations about all of this. I mean, besides the tents and the whole thing where we are probably going to end up ruining our host family's chances of getting decent housing, there is the fact that they have separated the girls' tents from the boys' tents with – I shudder to write it – Port-O-Lets!

Yes!!!!! That is right!!!!!! There are no working toilets! There are not even any indoor toilets – at least until we install our host family's. We have to use Port-O-Lets! And don't even get me started on the whole shower thing. The need for solar shower bags came into startling clarity when I saw the shower area, which is just a bunch of tarped-off stalls with hooks to hang your shower bag from.

And it looks like it's going to be Wet Wipes the whole way, as it is drizzling steadily and there is not a hint of sun.

The bell again. Got to go. Must find a place to hide this journal so the bears/serial killers/Lana won't find it while I am gone.

I really should try to get used to all this because if I ever want to volunteer with Greenpeace and help save the whales, the living conditions could be even worse.

Saturday, March 12, 9 p.m.,
Hominy Knob, West Virginia

We met our host family. They are Angie and Todd Harmeyer and their two children, three-year-old Mitchell and two-year-old Bubbah. I swear that is the baby's name. Bubbah. There is another baby on the way, too. Mrs Harmeyer is due in a month, though if you ask me, she looks like she could blow at any moment.

Mrs Harmeyer has a job sweeping up hair at a beauty salon in downtown Hominy Knob, which consists of a grocery store, a credit union, a hardware store, a consignment shop and the beauty salon. Mr Harmeyer has been unemployed since the local rubber tyre factory burned down. Both Mr and Mrs Harmeyer are very excited about their new house. They have been living in a trailer since they got married. Mitchell is especially excited about the prospect of having his own room. Right now, he has to sleep in the same bed as his mom and dad.

After we met the Harmeyers, and we were all standing in line to get our dinner – salad, corn on the cob, sloppy joes (being a vegetarian, I just took a bun and some of the vegetables) and string beans, and cherry cobbler, for dessert – Mrs Harmeyer asked me if it was true about my being a princess and the tall guy behind me being my bodyguard, and I said it was true.

'Well, whatchoo doin' spendin' your Spring Break around here, then, if you're a princess?' Mrs Harmeyer wanted to know. 'If I were a princess, I'd spend my Spring Break in Cabo San Lucas, ridin' on one of them jet skis.'

I explained to Mrs Harmeyer that I had been compelled to join Housing for the Homeless instead of spending my Spring Break riding on jet skis out of a keen sense of civic duty and a desire to help the needy.

Mrs Harmeyer just looked at me funny and went, 'What?'

So then I thought I had better change the subject, and asked Mrs Harmeyer if she knew the sex of her unborn child yet. Mrs Harmeyer surprised me by saying she didn't want to know, since if it was another boy, she knew she'd never push.

I was shocked to hear a woman in West Virginia echoing the exact same thing my mom back in New York City is always saying, and I asked Mrs Harmeyer if she, like my mom, was an opponent to the cult of the patriarchy, to which Mrs Harmeyer replied, 'Gosh, no, I just want somebody I can buy Barbies instead of G.I. Joes fer.'

After informing Mrs Harmeyer that I fully understood her feelings, I took my food and went and sat down by Michael. Lilly was at our table, too, filming everyone. She filmed Lana's fit when Dr Gonzales took her aside and told her leather miniskirts were not appropriate for the dining tent and that she would have to go back to her tent and change. She filmed all the young Hominy Knob girls who flocked around Josh the minute Lana went off in a huff to change her skirt, asking if he worked out and what kind of car he drove and if he lived in a penthouse in Noo Yor-rick. She filmed all the Hominy Knob locals who filed curiously past our table, pausing occasionally to ask me where my tiara was (answer: 'Back in New York'), what it felt like to be a princess ('OK') and why on earth I'd come to Hominy Knob ('To achieve self-actualization through selflessly helping others').

After dinner, Lilly declared she had enough footage for a mini-series, let alone a single episode of her show. She decided she was going to have to a do month-long tribute to Hominy Knob on her cable access show. She decided to call the documentary, *Sour Mash and Medicaid: The Failure of the Federal Government to Ease the Burden of the Rural Poor*.

It will, she says, bring the current administration to its knees.

After dinner, Dr Gonzales talked for a while, but I didn't pay much attention because I was thinking about the Port-O-Lets. Now I know why we'd been instructed to bring flashlights. There are no lights in the Port-O-Lets, so if you have to go in the middle of the night, you have to use your flashlight to see by. What's more, there's no telling what else might be sharing that Port-O-Let with you. I mean, if you ask me, it's the perfect hangout for spiders, possibly black widow spiders, whose bite can be deadly. At least according to the Discovery Channel.

I am definitely bringing my insect repellant with me to the bathroom every time I have to go.

It was after Dr Gonzales's long, boring talk that things really started to look up. That's because, walking back to our tents, Michael took my hand (it was dark, so no one saw), then pulled me behind a tree and started kissing me in a highly romantic manner. It definitely took my mind off the Port-O-Lets for a little while.

Nobody caught us, either . . . unlike Lana and Josh, who got fully busted making out behind the supply tent.

See, it totally pays to date a genius. They know where all the good makeout spots are.

Oh, no. The 'lights out' bell. We have to turn out our flashlights now, and go to sleep. I don't know how anyone can be expected to sleep out here in the wilderness. There are all sorts of weird noises, like hooting owls and crickets and stuff. At least we don't have to worry about bears, though. Lars opened his duffel bag and pulled out a pup tent, complete with an inflatable air mattress, and set it up right in front of our door. While this will make going to the Port-O-Let in the middle of the night slightly difficult – and will also, sadly, discourage any nocturnal visitations from boys – it makes me happy to know that Lars is out there with his Glock 9 mm and his numbchucks . . . even if he, like the rest of us, can't sleep due to the incredibly noisy owls.

I miss Manhattan already. What I wouldn't give to be lulled to sleep by the dulcet tones of a car alarm.

Sunday, March 13, noon, The dining tent

Oh, my God, every inch of me is sore. It is no joke trying to sleep on the ground. And the sides of our tent kept flapping all night, and I thought it was the Blair Witch trying to get in.

Plus when we woke up, everything was drenched with dew. DEW. There is no dew in New York City. Pigeons, maybe. Lots of rats. But no dew.

Dew is my new enemy.

It doesn't help that all I've done all morning is hold up wood frames. Apparently I am hopeless at hammering, sawing, drilling *and* pouring cement. Good thing I came all the way to West Virginia to find that out.

So I was in charge of holding up the wood frames while other people hammered them in, a task that requires no skill whatsoever, just plenty of upper body strength . . . which I am of course lacking, but I am not about to admit it to anyone. At least, not out loud.

Still, those frames are HEAVY! I mean, building houses is no joke.

Thank God for Michael, Lars, Dr Gonzales and Peter Tsu. I don't mean to be sexist, but at this point in the building stage, the guys are definitely doing a better job than the girls. Although Tina has proven to be pretty adept with the nail gun (lucky duck). I am pretty sure she is just doing it to look good in front of Peter Tsu, who has surprisingly shapely forearms – as Lilly was quick to point out, then film for posterity. Peter is almost as hot as Mulan's boyfriend, and he has the added bonus of not being a cartoon character.

Nobody could be hotter than my boyfriend, though. I just wish it were sunnier so Michael would get all sweaty and have to take his shirt off. That would make building a house WAY fun.

Well, that and actually knowing I was contributing to its construction in some meaningful way.

Anyway, our house is going up more quickly than anyone else's, despite our great handicap: Boris. While I am in no real way *helping* to build our house, at least I am not making things worse, the way Boris is. So far he has had two asthma attacks thanks to all the sawdust, and dropped a cinderblock on his foot (it will be all right, it is just bruised, Dr Gonzales says). We have now assigned him to keeping Mitchell and Bubbah from wandering too close to the chain saw, and refilling everybody's Gatorade containers.

Oh, yeah. I know why the Gatorade is so important now. Building a house is VERY tiring. You have to replace your electrolytes constantly.

Mr Harmeyer says beer is better for replacing electrolytes than Gatorade, but Dr Gonzales pointed out to him that alcohol dehydrates the body very quickly, and after that, Mr Harmeyer shut up.

Oh, and Lana got sent back to her tent after she arrived at her worksite wearing a tube top with low rise jeans. Her face, when Dr Gonzales told her she'd have to go back and change, was a picture. It reminded me of the time the Albert Einstein High School junior varsity cheerleaders were doing basket tosses and somebody forgot to spot Lana and she ended up breaking off the tip of her coccyx bone and the doctors couldn't find it and Lilly did that spoof on her TV show called *Travels With Lana's Coccyx Bone*, showing how Lana's coccyx bone was moving through Lana's bloodstream, visiting with the other bones, and stuff.

Lunch is salad, cornbread, mashed potatoes and pork tenderloin sandwiches. I am just having salad and mashed potatoes. I am sick of corn already, though I understand that it is a staple of the West Virginian diet, like bagels and smoked salmon are in New York.

Sunday, March 13, 9 p.m., The tent

Too tired to give full account of day. Just held up more wood frames. For hours.

Dinner: salad, Tater Tots, hamburgers, corn. Just ate salad and Tater Tots. Sight of corn makes me want to puke.

Fell asleep during inspirational speech by Dr Gonzales. Woke up with head on Michael's shoulder. He was very nice about it. Hope I didn't drool.

Josh and Lana caught making out behind shower area. Sadly am too tired to make out with own boyfriend. Am going to sleep right now, too exhausted to wait for lights out.

Monday, March 14, noon, The dining tent

Woke to full-on rain. Wet Wipes instead of showers for everyone. That's OK, my muscles would have been too sore to carry my five-gallon solar shower-bag to shower area anyway. Besides, the dew soaked through my sleeping bag, right down to my pyjamas. I feel like I've already had a shower.

Fortunately, we had already framed in the roof of the Harmeyers's house. Spent morning applying gypsum board to interior walls. Will shingle roof later if rain lets up. May be getting better at this house building thing, hammer only went through gypsum board five times. Mrs Harmeyer says that's OK, she can hang pictures over holes. But Michael says no, we will plaster over them.

Lana sent back to tent to change after appearing at worksite wearing leopard print body stocking under cut-off jean shorts. I suppose she got hit on the head yesterday and thought she was Christina Aguilera.

Lunch is turkey sandwiches, potato salad, Jell-O and corn chips. Ate potato salad and Jell-O.

Aw, geez, back to work.

Monday, March 14, 10 p.m., The tent

Too tired to write much. Rain let up and spent afternoon on roof shingling with Lilly, Tina and Peter Tsu. Only fell off roof once. Landed on Boris, so that was all right. Michael, Lars, and Dr Gonzales installed the plumbing. Mrs Harmeyer cried when her toilet flushed for the first time. It was a deeply moving moment.

After dinner – salad, fried chicken, creamed corn and rolls (only ate salad and rolls) – Michael and I volunteered to 'inventory the tools' in the supply tent.

Except that when we got there, it turned out the supply tent was already occupied, but not by Lana and Josh . . . by Mr Wheeton and Mademoiselle Klein, no less!!!!

They made us swear not to tell anyone. We said we wouldn't if they wouldn't tell anyone on us. After they agreed and went away, Michael and I had a very romantic interlude in the supply tent that was tragically cut short when I felt something crawling up my leg and looked down and saw the world's biggest bug on my calf. I screamed so loud that Lars came bursting in with his gun drawn.

Michael said it was only a centipede.

ONLY A CENTIPEDE? IT TOUCHED MY SKIN!!!!!!!!!

It is much easier to be an environmentalist when you live in the city where there aren't that many bugs than when you are in the country and are being eaten alive by them. I am not sure I love nature as much as I used to think I did.

Tuesday, March 15, noon, The dining tent

Worked all morning, still so much left to do, and this is LAST DAY. But still must paint all walls and trim, too, plus install flooring, etc. Boris dropped a shutter on his big toe, but Dr Gonzales said it isn't broken, just dislocated. He manipulated it back into place – I would so never touch Boris's feet. Dr Gonzales is truly a saint – and buddy-taped it to the toe next to it so it would stay where it is supposed to.

Mrs Harmeyer complaining of heartburn since breakfast, but no one else is feeling sick. Legionnaires' disease ruled out as we have been dining al fresco. Possibly result of two Diet Cokes she downed with her eggs and bacon? Unborn child could be a phenylketonuric. Warned Mrs Harmeyer about dangers of too much aspartame. It is a good thing I have watched so many episodes of *A Baby Story* on the Learning Channel in preparation for the arrival of my new baby brother or sister. I am truly a font of pre-natal information.

Tuesday, March 15, 9 p.m.,
Last day of Home Building

So tired, but truly amazing day, must get it all down before I forget:

Finished building Mr and Mrs Harmeyer's house. When we were done, we all stood around and marvelled: we had built a three-bedroomed, one-bathroomed house in three days, complete with kitchen, dining room and family room. I mean, it is not a BIG house (only 1,200 square feet, smaller than our loft) and it isn't like the Harmeyers can afford cable or Ikea furniture or anything. But it is a house, not a double wide, like Mitchell and Bubbah have been living in their whole lives.

And you know, it didn't look so bad. I mean, we had plastered over the holes I'd made in the gypsum board, so you couldn't even see them. And with the vinyl siding, it looked, I don't know, like a REAL house.

While we were standing there admiring our handiwork, Mrs Harmeyer complained that she had a wicked case of heartburn and had anyone else had the potato salad at lunch? I informed Mrs Harmeyer that, being a vegetarian, I had eaten nothing but potato salad for lunch, as it had been the only non-meat dish available, and that I felt fine. Then I opened my diary to the entry I wrote earlier today and showed Mrs Harmeyer that she had complained of indigestion after breakfast, as well. Was it possible, I asked, that she wasn't having heartburn at all, but contractions? The two have occasionally been confused, even by experienced mothers, at least according to *A Baby Story*.

Then Mrs Harmeyer got all excited and yelled, 'Oh my God! Todd, git the pickup!'

So Mr and Mrs Harmeyer sped off for the hospital, leaving us in charge of Mitchell and Bubbah. Dr Gonzales was way impressed by what he called my 'powers of observation'. Not everybody, he said, would have kept such a detailed record of another person's complaints about their gastritis.

I told Dr Gonzales that it was no big deal, that I write down everything, really. Then he said the funniest thing. He said: 'That's quite a skill.'

Wow! It almost made me think maybe being able to write isn't such a bad talent, after all! I mean, it isn't as cool as being able to use a nail gun, and all. But hey, it might not be *totally* useless.

Then Dr Gonzales turned to Michael and said, 'We're out of hot dog buns for the celebration barbecue tonight. If I stay here with Mitchell and Bubbah, do you think you could go into town and pick some up?' And he handed Michael the keys to his Dodge Chevy!

And it turns out Michael can drive! He has a driver's licence and everything! He learned two summers ago at his parents' country house in Albany.

There are very few boys who live in Manhattan who know how to drive, on account of hardly anyone owning a car in New York City.

So Michael said, 'Sure, Dr Gonzales,' and then we all tried not to whoop too loudly as me, Lars, Lilly, Boris, Tina and Peter Tsu piled into the truck and peeled out for town.

Town was a big disappointment, though. I'd forgotten that Mrs Harmeyer had said there was nothing to do in it. There is not even a single Chinese restaurant where you can go for cold sesame noodles. We went to the grocery store and got the hot dog buns, and Lilly was all, 'Finally, I can get a bagel!' but they didn't even have any, not even the Thomas's kind in a bag.

So then we were all kind of depressed on account of the no bagel and no cold sesame noodle thing. But when we got back in the truck, Michael went, 'Well, there's one thing West Virginia has that Manhattan doesn't,' and he started driving.

I thought Michael was talking about the Mothman, you know, from that movie, and I couldn't think what was so great about that because all the Mothman does is call people on the phone and say in a scary voice, 'Stay away from the chemical plant!' which isn't really useful information to anyone.

But it turns out Michael wasn't talking about the Mothman. He was talking about Dairy Queen! Yes! It turns out there was a Diary Queen right outside Hominy Knob! There are no Dairy Queens in Manhattan, except for a gross one nobody but tourists ever go to in Penn Station.

We were so excited, we piled out of the truck and rushed up to the girl in the window. Everybody got something different. Lars got a cherry slush. Lilly got a peanut buster parfait. Boris got a Heath Bar bite blizzard. Peter Tsu got a Coke slush. Tina got low-cal yogurt on account of the fact that Peter Tsu was looking. Michael got an Oreo cookie blizzard. I got a chocolate dipped vanilla swirl.

And it was SO good! After all our hard work, and the sleeping in tents and the Port-O-Lets and the Wet Wipes and finding out that I actually have a useful talent after all, that chocolate dipped vanilla swirl was really the most delicious thing I had ever eaten in my whole life.

We were all enjoying our ice cream, leaning against the side of the Dodge Chevy in the soft spring sunshine, when this other truck pulled up next to ours, and Josh and Lana and some other people from the popular crowd piled out. They had, it became clear, borrowed their host family's car.

'Oh, God,' Lana said, when she saw us. 'What are YOU doing here? There's another Dairy Queen in Smoot Gap down the road.' Lana jerked her thumb in that direction. 'You guys go there.'

'I don't think so,' Peter Tsu said. 'We got here first.'

Lana nearly spontaneously combusted at that one. Apparently she thought that her position as queen of the social scene of Albert Einstein High School extended all the way down to West Virginia.

'Oh,' she said, narrowing her eyes at us. 'When we get back to school, you are so dead.'

'Don't you think,' Lilly said, 'that this is a little childish, Lana? Are you really just going to ignore everything we've learned these past few days about loving your fellow man, and try to make us go to Smoot Gap because you can't stand to be at the same Dairy Queen as us?'

'Uh,' Lana said. 'Yeah.'

'Lana,' I said. 'Dairy Queen, like Housing for the Homeless, has an open-door policy: anyone who wants to enjoy soft serve can, regardless of religious preference, ethnic or economic background, or position in the social hierarchy of their high school. Popular kids *and* dorks, eating ice cream together.'

Lana sucked in her breath. 'Josh!' she cried. 'Don't just stand there! Do something!'

Josh took his hands out of his pockets and said, 'You heard the lady.' He reached out and shoved Michael in the shoulder. 'Get back in the truck and clear out.'

'Why don't you?' Michael said, shoving Josh right back.

Who knows what would have happened next if at that very moment, a large black limo hadn't slithered into the Dairy Queen parking lot? All I knew was, Michael and Josh were both still wearing their tool belts (and sadly their shirts). It was entirely possible that the 'theology of the hammer' could have taken on a whole new meaning right then and there!!!!!

Fortunately it didn't come to that because a) Lars would have put a stop to it before that happened, and b) the door to the limo opened, and the person who got out of it looked so out of place for Hominy Knob that everyone stopped what they were doing and just stood there, staring.

'Grandmere!' I cried, barely able to believe my eyes.

'Amelia,' Grandmere said, looking around in

distaste. She was dressed in a big feathered purple velvet coat, with Rommel in one arm and a purse in the other. All the residents of Hominy Knob who happened to be in the vicinity could not take their eyes off her. 'You're looking . . . fit.'

'Grandmere,' I said. 'What are you doing here? I thought you were going to Palm Springs.'

'I did go there. I thought I would stop by to see you on my way home. I've been to your, er, work-site.'

'Really?' I was still shocked to see Grandmere in Hominy Knob. 'Did you see the house we built?'

'I did,' Grandmere said. 'I must admit, when you told me this is what you wanted to do with your Spring Break, I thought you were mad. But I met Dr Gonzales, and he seems like a very nice man. And your house is . . . adequate. That is not, however, why I am here. I've taken rooms at the Hampton Inn – sadly, the finest quarters I was able to procure. I thought perhaps you might all like to come back with me and shower before your little celebration dinner, to which Dr Gonzales has very kindly invited me. I understand the bathing conditions at the camp are on the primitive side, and all of you have a very long bus ride ahead of you tomorrow.'

We all started piling back into the truck without another word. Lana and her friends did, too, but Grandmere just looked at her and went, 'Oh, no, not you, dear. The offer is really only for Amelia and her *friends*.'

Then she got back into the limo without another word.

I felt really sorry for Lana. NOT.

So we all followed Grandmere's limo to the motel, where she'd taken seven rooms for herself and Rommel, her bodyguards, her personal maid, her assistant, her driver and her clothes. Everybody got to take a nice long hot shower and use some clean towels for a change. After we had washed away all the sawdust and dew, we thanked Grandmere and said we had to be going back to camp in order to deliver the hot dog buns.

When we got there, we found out that Mrs Harmeyer had given birth to a healthy eight-pound baby girl. But what REALLY blew me away was when Dr Gonzales said, 'And, Mia, the Harmeyers said to tell you that they named her after you.'

'Really?' I was flattered. 'They named their baby Mia?'

Dr Gonzales looked uncomfortable. 'Uh,' he said. 'Not exactly. They named her Princess.'

Princess Harmeyer. Oh, well. It's still nice to know I have left my mark on Hominy Knob. Sort of.

After the celebration dinner – which was really nice; they seemed to have run out of corn products – we all gathered around the campfire Dr Gonzales had built, and toasted marshmallows. Michael got out his guitar and we all sang that Kumbaya song, the one that makes me feel like crying every time I hear it.

Then to show our West Virginian hosts some New York City flava Lilly and Tina and I sang our version of Destiny Child's 'Survivor', which we do very well (Lilly even let me be Beyoncé for a change). Grandmere clapped like crazy, even though Lana snorted several times and Lars laughed so hard that he almost choked on a s'more and Mrs Hill had to smack him on the back.

Then the host families sang a West Virginian song that was very sad, about a girl who may have been born poor white trash, but Fancy was her name. It was all about how Fancy used her talents to get ahead in life. She never complained about having the WRONG KIND of talent, she just used what God gave her. That, I realized, is what *I* need to start doing: stop wishing for better talents, and just learn to use the one I have to the best of my ability.

I sighed pretty hard when I thought of this, and Michael must have thought I was sad or something, since he put his arm around me.

Then we had some nice passionate moments near his tent while he was supposed to be putting his guitar away.

Afterwards I went back to the campfire to say goodnight to Grandmere. Only I didn't get a chance to. Because she was busy making out with Dr Gonzales!

MY GRANDMOTHER!!!!!!! AND DR GONZALES!!!!!!!!

I couldn't believe it. But I guess it is just another example of the theology of the hammer at work.

Wednesday, March 16, 10 p.m., The Loft

I am home!!!!!!!!! AT LAST!!!!!!!!!!

The bus ride back from West Virginia was SO much better than the bus ride there. For one thing, Principal Gupta made sure Boris was good and dosed with Dramamine before she let him anywhere near the parking lot. And then everybody was so tired, they all fell asleep before we even got on to Highway 64.

When the bus finally pulled up in front of Albert Einstein High School, and everyone started piling off to collect their bags from Charlie, there was a lot of hugging and 'See you Monday's going on from people who before the trip hadn't been friends. Like between us and Peter Tsu.

None of us hugged Lana, though. The theology of the hammer does not extend THAT far.

The funniest part was, right before the bus left Hominy Knob, Dr Gonzales came up to me and, looking all embarrassed, went, 'Princess Mia, please tell your grandmother that I enjoyed meeting her very much. She is truly a dynamic woman.'

Ha! Dr Gonzales has no idea HOW dynamic Grandmere can be. He probably doesn't even suspect that he is just another one in a long string of men she has conquered with her own God-given talents . . . whatever those might be.

I am so happy to be home, I ran around kissing everything I'd missed, including Fat Louie, the mattress on my bed, my bath tub, the refrigerator and the TV.

But most of all I kissed my mom, and told her that even though West Virginia is all right and everything, it is really true what Dorothy says in *The Wizard of Oz*, about there being no place like home.

'Even if you're on Spring Break?' my mom wanted to know.

'Even if you're on Spring Break,' I said.

'Even if you're a princess?' my mom asked.

'*Especially* if you're a princess,' I said.

And then I picked up the phone and called Number One Noodle Son and ordered us all some cold sesame noodles for dinner.

The PRINCESS MIA SLEEPOVER BEAUTY BAG for 6 contains:

5 Beauty Bags up for grabs plus the first 1,000 entries will get a free sparkly nail varnish

6 pairs of Princess Mia pyjamas
A bag full of make-up
A copy of The Princess Diaries video
6 copies of your very own diary
A Princess superstar quiz & cool games
& loads of fashion and gossip magazines.

See the back cover of this book for details of how to enter this competition and join The Princess Diaries Princess Club

TXT
07950 080700